Snowden,
Raggedy Ann and Andy's
Christmas Eve Adventure

LITTLE SIMON

An imprint of Simon & Schuster Children's Publishing Division

1230 Avenue of the Americas New York, New York 10020

Copyright © 1998 Simon & Schuster

Snowden and Friends™ and © 1998 Dayton Hudson Corporation.

All rights reserved. Raggedy Ann and Raggedy Andy used under license

with Simon & Schuster Children's Publishing Division.

The names and depictions of Raggedy Ann and Raggedy Andy

are trademarks of Simon & Schuster, Inc.

LITTLE SIMON and colophon are registered trademarks of Simon & Schuster.

Manufactured in the United States of America

First Edition 10 9 8 7 6 5 4 3 2 1

ISBN 0-689-82368-1

Snowden,
Raggedy Ann and Andy's
Christmas Eve Adventure

BY TINA WILCOX
ILLUSTRATED BY CRAIG CARL

LITTLE SIMON

The day before Christmas was baking day at Grandma's house, and every year Marcella came to help. Grandma was waiting for her when Marcella ran up the steps.

"Merry Almost-Christmas, Grandma!" Marcella sang out as she ran into Grandma's open arms. She smelled cinnamon and pine needles and pumpkin pie coming from inside the house.

"And Merry Almost-Christmas to you, Marcella," replied her grandmother. "I hope you came ready to work, because we have a lot of baking to do today. Come, let's get in out of this cold air."

"Well, look who's here!" said Grandma with a smile as they walked into the kitchen. "I didn't know I was getting *three* helpers today!"

"Raggedy Ann and Andy came along to watch, Grandma," responded Marcella. "They know we have a lot to do today and promised they wouldn't get in the way."

"Then I'll just set them down where they can see us," Grandma said.

"Now, Marcella, why don't you start mixing the dough for the sugar cookies while I take the first batch of gingerbread snowmen out of the oven. When they're cool enough, we'll decorate them."

"Yes, Grandma. Can we bake peanut butter cookies today, too?" Marcella asked.

"We can bake all the cookies we want to, as long as they are ready in time for Christmas dinner tomorrow," replied Grandma. "So let's get to work."

It was late in the day and Grandma and Marcella were almost done baking. Grandma looked at all the goodies.

"It seems to me we're ready for Christmas," said Grandma.

"But we still need to decorate the snowman cookies," replied Marcella.

"You're right," Grandma said, "but we're out of sugar."

Grandma put on her coat. "I'll borrow a cup of sugar from Mrs. Adams across the road. Sometimes she can be quite a talker, though, so it may take a while."

"Okay, Grandma," replied Marcella. "I'll play outside until you come back."

Marcella went outside and looked around.

"This snow would be perfect for making a snowman," she said to herself. "I'll build one to surprise Grandma." So she rolled together three big balls of snow.

She placed one on top of the other.

Then she patted snow onto the sides to make arms, and drew a smile on his face with a stick. She used an icicle as a nose.

Marcella put two buttons
on the snowman's head to
create his eyes.

She then put on a vest,
two mittens, and a hat
that she had borrowed
from a box of old clothes
in Grandma's attic.

"Arms, nose, eyes, and
smile," said Marcella. "What
a wonderful snowman you
are!" She kissed him on his
snowy cheek.

"Why, Marcella, what a lovely snowman," Grandma said when she returned. "Let's get back inside and ice those snowman cookies. Now we know exactly what they should look like!"

After dinner Grandma said, "I have a surprise for you, Marcella. Bring Raggedy Ann and Andy to my sewing room, and I'll show you."

Grandma opened a box on her sewing table and pulled out two small Christmas outfits for Raggedy Ann and Andy.

"They're wonderful!" said Marcella. Just as she finished putting the clothes on the dolls, Marcella's mother arrived. Marcella hugged her grandmother and ran out, leaving the dolls behind.

Grandma turned off all the lights and went to bed. In a dark corner next to her sewing table, Raggedy Ann and Andy lay jumbled in a heap. Without a sound, they tiptoed through the house to the front room where they climbed up onto a chair and slipped out an open window onto the front porch.

The dolls sat on the porch steps.

"Marcella forgot us again," said Raggedy Andy with a sigh.

"Yes," said Raggedy Ann. "And I was really looking forward to spending Christmas morning with her."

"Me, too," replied Raggedy Andy, "but we won't this year."

"No, nobody will be thinking about us on Christmas," said Raggedy Ann.

Just then a gentle little voice said, "I'm thinking about you and it isn't even Christmas!"

Raggedy Ann and Andy looked up to find the snowman Marcella had made standing in front of them.

"Who are you?" asked Raggedy Ann and Andy together.

"I'm Snowden," said the snowman with a smile. "And I'm here to help you get back home."

"Why, thank you, Snowden! Can we be home before Marcella opens her presents in the morning?" Raggedy Andy asked.

"We can try!" replied Snowden. "But first we have to figure out which path to take."

Raggedy Ann picked up a stick and started drawing in the snow. "If we travel by road it would take too long," she said. "But if we took a shortcut through the woods, we would have much less distance to cover. We would need light, though, to help us find the way, so maybe we should wait until the sun comes up."

Snowden shivered. "If you don't mind, I'd prefer to travel by night," he said. "You see, when the sun shines, I start to melt."

"Then it's settled!" said Raggedy Andy. "We'll head for home through the woods and get there before sunrise!"

And with that, Snowden and Raggedy Ann and Andy set off.

Snowden led the way into the snowy woods.
After they had walked for a while, Raggedy
Andy pointed up into a tree. "Look! An owl!"
Snowden replied, "Many animals come out at
night. The woods are beautiful, don't you think?"
"Yes," replied Raggedy Ann, "but I'd rather be at home
on Christmas eve."
Snowden stopped suddenly and pointed to
footprints in the snow.
"Look at these!" he said. "We have company."
"Oh, no! Those footprints are ours!" said Raggedy Ann.
"We've gotten turned around. Now we'll never get home in
time for Christmas."

Just then Raggedy Andy heard a tiny voice. "Hello, strangers. May I help you?"

Raggedy Andy replied, "Yes, please, Mr. Gray Mouse. Can you tell us how to get to Marcella's house?"

"Hmm, let me see," replied Mr. Gray Mouse. "No, I don't know. But then again I don't travel very far from home. I have too many little ones to look after. See what I mean?"

They looked under a ledge and found Mrs. Gray Mouse and her sleeping mouse children.

"How sweet!" said Raggedy Ann.

"Back to your question," said Mr. Gray Mouse. "I don't know where Marcella's house is, but Mrs. Redbird might. See that tall tree on top of Redbird Hill? Just tap on the tree trunk three times. Now if you'll excuse me, I still have four stockings to hang for Santa Claus. Good night, and I hope you find your way!"

And with that, Mr. Gray Mouse turned and trotted back into his home under the snow.

The trio walked up to the tree, then Raggedy Andy tapped on the trunk. Instantly Mrs. Redbird fluttered out from among the branches.

"What's happening?" she cried. "Is someone chopping down my tree?"

Snowden took off his hat and bowed like a perfect snowy gentleman. "I am sorry to disturb you on Christmas Eve, Mrs. Redbird, but I am trying to help my two friends find their way home for Christmas. Mr. Gray Mouse said you might know how to get to Marcella's house."

Before Mrs.
Redbird could answer,
Mr. Redbird and the two Redbird
boys appeared.

"Mother, is that Santa and his
elves?" asked one of the boys.

"No," said Mrs. Redbird, "these are
some travelers lost in the woods, and I
am trying to help them. Now go back
to bed and when you wake up, it will
be Christmas Day."

As soon as Mr. Redbird and his sons left Snowden whispered to Mrs. Redbird, "Can you really help us find the way?"

"Well," chirped Mrs. Redbird, "the moon is bright and the sky is clear, my eyes are sharp and I can fly above the trees, so all I need to know is what I'm looking for."

Raggedy Ann said, "Marcella lives in a house at the bottom of a hill. There's a big spruce tree in the front yard with red and green Christmas lights on its' branches and a gold star on top."

"Sounds easy enough," said Mrs. Redbird. "I'll be right back!" And without another word, she flew up into the sky. "There it is!" she said, pointing with her wing, "If you head straight down the hill, you'll find your way home!"

After thanking Mrs. Redbird, the trio were on their way.

When they reached the edge of the woods, Snowden looked up into the sky. "Oh, no! The sun is rising," he said.

"Quick!" said Raggedy Ann. "Let's run down the hill as fast as we can!"

The sun felt warm as the friends hurried down the hill.

"Hurry! Faster!" cried Raggedy Andy as he pulled Snowden with him.

By the time the three of them reached Marcella's house at the bottom of the hill, Snowden had almost completely melted.

Raggedy Ann knelt down and said, "Snowden, please stay with us. We're home in time for Christmas, but it won't be any fun if you're not with us."

Snowden whispered, "I'm so glad you'll celebrate Christmas with Marcella. Don't forget the great adventure we had together or your friend, Snowden."

A few minutes later when Marcella opened the front door to let her cat in, she found Raggedy Ann and Andy lying in a jumble on the front porch.

"Oh, no! You two must have fallen out of my backpack last night when I came home!" said Marcella. Let's go inside You're just in time to open the Christmas presents!"

Christmas morning was full of love and laughter. Marcella thought it was the best Christmas ever.

Raggedy Ann and Raggedy Andy had fun, too, but every now and then they looked out the window at the snowy hillside and remembered their friend, Snowden.

Later in the day Marcella pulled on her coat, picked up Raggedy Ann and Andy, and went outdoors.

"Brrrr, it's gotten colder," said Marcella.

As she walked around the corner of the house, she came across a hat, a pair of mittens, and an old vest.

"That's funny," she said, "how did these get here?" When she picked them up, she found two buttons on the snow.

Suddenly Marcella got an idea. "I know! I'll build another snowman—a special Christmas snowman—and I'll use these things!" she said.

So Marcella rolled together
three big balls of snow. She
placed one on top of the other.

Then she patted snow
onto the sides, and drew
a smile on his face. She
used an icicle as a nose.

Then she put the clothes on him.
"What a wonderful snowman
you are!" Marcella said.
Grandma arrived just then.
They hugged and went inside
to have Christmas dinner.

Late that night Marcella was sound asleep after a long and happy Christmas day. Raggedy Ann and Andy quietly slipped out of bed and looked out the window. There in the snowy moonlight stood the snowman.

"Doesn't he look a lot like Snowden?" asked Raggedy Andy.

"Yes," replied Raggedy Ann with a smile. "In fact as we were returning to the house, I heard him whisper something."

"What did he say?" asked Raggedy Andy eagerly.

Raggedy Ann giggled. "He said, 'Hello, my friend. Is it time to have another adventure?'"